# Contents

|   |                    | Page |
|---|--------------------|------|
| 1 | Jez                | 1    |
| 2 | A New Image        | 3    |
| 3 | Shopping           | 7    |
| 4 | The Credit Card    | 11   |
| 5 | New Clothes        | 14   |
| 6 | The Post           | 18   |
| 7 | 'Oh Lucy'          | 21   |
| 8 | The School Party   | 27   |

# 1

## Jez

---

'Jez fancies you, Lucy,' said Jenna.

'Jez?'

'Yeah,' said Jenna.

'How do you know?' I asked.

'He's been asking about you.
What you're like.
Where you live.
That sort of stuff.'

I could feel myself going red.
'What did you tell him?' I asked.

'Not much,' she said.
'It's best if he finds out for himself.
Isn't it?'

My face was on fire.
Jez Cooper fancied me,
Lucy Snedden.
Wow.
I don't fancy him.
He's a bit of a prat,
but I'm pleased he fancies me.
Pleased to bits.

# 2

# A New Image

Snip.
A curl of my hair fell to the ground.
Clip.
Two curls of hair fell down.
Cut, snip, clip.

'Steady on Jenna,' I cried.

'Relax, Lucy.
Sit back in your chair.
You're going to look so cool,'
said Jenna.

'I don't want it too short,' I said.

Jenna cut away.
More of my hair fell to the ground.
A minute later she'd finished.
'Now you can look in the mirror,'
she said.

I opened one eye and then the other.
A new me with spiky hair
was clear to see.

'It's a bit short,' I said.

'It's amazing,' said Jenna.
'You wanted a new image.
Now you've got one.
Jez will love it.'

'Will he?' I asked.

'Oh yeah,' said Jenna.
'You just wait and see Lucy.'

Next day at school I smiled at Jez.
'Hi,' I said.
Jez didn't smile back or grin at me.
Instead, he looked away and ran off.
'My hair is a disaster,' I told Jenna.

'No, no,' she said.
'Your hair is wicked.
You just need some new clothes.

'You need a neat style
to go with your neat hair.
Then Jez will go wild about you.'

'Will he?'

'Oh yeah. You wait and see,'
said Jenna.

It was fine for Jenna to talk
about new clothes,
and to say I needed a neat style.
It was great for her to tell me that Jez would
go wild about me.
A new image doesn't come cheap.
How was I ever going to get any cash
to buy new stuff?

# 3
# Shopping

I looked ay myself in the mirror.
A big long mirror.
My clothes were fine.
Comfortable.
They weren't new.
They weren't neat.
They were a bit baggy maybe.
But they were me.
I felt good in them.

Jenna came round and we went into town.
'I haven't any cash to buy anything,'
I told her.
Jenna goes to town every Saturday.
Big time shopping.
Most Saturdays I go swimming
with my brother.
Blue water splashing in my face
gave way to busy streets
and crowded shops.

Jenna was on a mission.
It was serious shopping time.
'Try this on Lucy,' she said,
grabbing a jacket from the clothes rack.

'There's no point.
I don't have any cash,' I said.

'And this . . . and this,' she said.
She wasn't listening to what I was saying.

She pushed a bundle of clothes
into my hands.
'Go to the fitting room.
Try them on,' she said.

I pushed them back towards her.
'I told you that I don't have any money.'

'Relax,' she said.
'Just try them on.
Nobody says you have to buy them.
It's only a bit of a giggle.'

Three minutes later I was back
by her side.
'That was quick,' she said.

'No good,' I lied.
'The jacket didn't fit and the trousers
made my bum look huge.
A total waste of time,' I told her.

Back at home I looked at myself
in the mirror again.
I wasn't comfortable any longer.
My old jeans looked old and tatty.
My sweat-shirt was ripped and frayed.
I ran my hands over my shoulders.
I could still feel the sleek smoothness
of the jacket in the shop.
So trim.
So cool.
I had to have it.

# 4
# The Credit Card

I held up the store credit card.
It had been stuffed in a drawer for ages.
Mum had never used it.
I turned it over in my hand.
It wasn't even signed.
I could get the jacket with that card.
It would just be the jacket -
nothing else.
I could pay mum back later.
My hand reached out for a pen.

I went to town after school,
on my own.
I changed out of my school uniform
in the ladies toilet.
I put some make-up on.
Anyone might think I was 18,
and old enough to have my own credit card.

The jacket was still on the rack.
There was just one left in my size.
My hand felt into my pocket.
My fingers gripped the edges
of the neat plastic shape.
It was so simple.
I lifted the jacket clear of the rack
and turned towards the payment point.

'Hello Lucy,' said a familiar voice.
I froze.

'Smart jacket you've got there.'
Jenna reached out to stroke it.

'You'll look a stunner
at the school party wearing that.
All the lads will fancy you.
You wait and see.'

At the payment point the woman
didn't even look at me.
I showed her the card
and signed with my mum's name.

'The boys won't be ignoring you now,'
said Jenna. 'You'll look like a star.'

# 5
## New Clothes

It wasn't enough.

The jacket looked cool, for sure.

It was a neat and sleek fit,

but the rest of my clothes were dreadful.

I couldn't go to a party in them.

No way.

I had to be a star.

I wanted to see all the lads staring at me.

I needed more new clothes.

I needed them until it hurt.

Shoes, jeans, socks.
Knitwear, silkwear, anywear.
Silky, shiny clothes.
Chunky, bobbly clothes.
There were clothes that fitted,
and others that didn't.
I bought the lot.

With slippery plastic carriers,
at least one in each hand,
I joined the throng of shoppers.
I danced down the streets.
I drank in the bright lights.
I gobbled up the buzz.
'Shop 'till you drop,
and then shop again.'
I was alive.

I had to wait until my mum was out
before I could bring my shopping home.
Then I got more daring.
I'd hear her in the kitchen
and sneak upstairs.
I'd climb up the stairs and make sure
I didn't tread on the creaking stair.
I'd lock my bedroom door behind me.
I'd stuff it all in my wardrobe,
until it was overflowing.
I'd hide it under my bed.
A secret is safe when its hidden away.

One day I wore a silky new top to school.
I hid it under my jacket when I left home.
When I walked into the classroom
all the lads stared.
Jez and Ben and Zak and Tariq.
They all had their mouths wide open.
Their chins practically bounced
off their work tables.

'That's not school uniform, Lucy.
Put your jacket back on immediately.'

Why do teachers have to spoil everything?
I had my jacket off
for less than five minutes,
but it was worth it.
It was worth every single second.

'Jez really does fancy you Lucy,'
said Jenna.

'I know,' I replied.

'So do Ben, Zak and Tariq,' said Jenna.

I beamed a huge smile.
It lasted the rest of the day.

# 6
## The Post

My mum was out when the post came.
She had two letters addressed to her.
I picked them both up off the floor
where they'd landed.
I wished I hadn't touched them.
I recognised the logo
on one of the letters.
It was the same logo that was
on the store credit card.
It was in a bright red colour.
Too bright.
Fire bright.
It was burning in my hand.

For ages I stood holding the letters.
I couldn't move.
I was unsure what to do next.
I put my fingernail under the corner
of the flap of the logo letter.
With just one flick I could open it
and see what was inside.
I could read how much I'd spent.
My fingernail was sharp,
but my brain was dull.

I lurched into the kitchen
and put one letter on the table.
I ripped the second into pieces.
Then ripped the pieces into tiny bits.
But the red brightness still shone out.

I raced into the lounge
and set fire to the bits in the fire grate.
The flames turned them all to grey ash.
I banged the poker on the ash
until it was dust.

# 7
## 'Oh Lucy'

It was the week of the school party.
Jenna and I were up in my bedroom.
We were trying on a load of clothes
that we might wear at the party.
We were having a real giggle.
We had music turned up loud –
wall to wall sound.

'What about these?' shouted Jenna
waving a pair of silky black trousers.

'Too tight,' I shouted back louder.

Then Jenna grabbed a very sparkly top.
'Oh Lucy,' she shouted.
'You must wear this.
You'll be so cool.
Try it on so I can see
what you'll look like.'

Before I could take the top from her
there was a shout from downstairs.
'Lucy,' called Mum.

Jenna turned the music up even louder
and began to dance about.
She was holding the sparkly top
as if she was dancing with it.
Mum shouted again.
'Lucy, I need to speak to you.'
The music almost drowned her out –
nearly, but not quite.
There was something strange
about her voice.

A few seconds later
I closed my bedroom door behind me.
I went downstairs.
Mum was standing
with a letter in her hand.
'We need to talk Lucy,' she said.

Jenna went home.
The music stopped.

Mum was looking me in the eyes.
'Have you been shopping?' she said.
'Did you use that old store credit card?
This letter has just come.
Is this anything to do with you?'

She put the letter into my hands.
It was the credit card bill, for £567.24.

For a minute I was going to lie
and say that I knew nothing about it.

I'd tell her that there must
be some mistake.
I'd tell her that
they'd got the wrong address.
But I caught mum's eye.

'These are things you've bought,
aren't they?' she said.

I nodded.

'Oh Lucy,' she said.
'How could you have done such a thing?'

'I'm sorry,' I stammered.

'Why didn't you tell me about it?'
she said.
I opened my mouth
but no words came out.
'I can never pay this bill,' she said.
'I simply don't have the money.'

# 8
# The School Party

I sit looking out of the window
at the black sky.
It's the night of the school party.
Jenna will be dancing.
Jez will be laughing.
Maybe he'll be dancing too.
And Ben and Zak and Tariq.
They'll be having a really wicked time.

Jenna said I must go.
She said it didn't matter
if I didn't have anything special to wear.
She even offered to lend me
some of her clothes.

My bedroom is empty.
All the new clothes have been sent
back to the shop.
But mum is still worrying
about the credit card bill.
Nothing has been finally sorted.
She may have to pay back some of it.

And me?
I'd sooner not talk about it.
Let's just say,
I won't be shopping for a while.